Who Did It?

By Francie Alexander

Illustrated by Jackie Snider

To Mom from Dad and Me

SCHOLASTIC INC.

New York Toronto London Auckland Sydney
Mexico City New Delhi Hong Kong Buenos Aires

Who made the pin?
Dad did.

Who put it in the bag?
I did.

Who made the tag?
I did.

Who hid it?
We did.

Who hid the milk?
Dad did.

Who hid the jam?
I did.

Who hid the pink rose?
We did.

Who will lift the napkin?
Mom!